P9-DIY-434

For
Kevin and Dawon,
hello and goodbye

Clarion Books
a Houghton Mifflin Company imprint
215 Park Avenue South, New York, NY 10003
Text and illustrations copyright © 1992 by David Wiesner
All rights reserved.
For information about permission to reproduce selections from
this book, write to Permissions, Houghton Mifflin Company,
215 Park Avenue South, New York, NY 10003.
Printed in the U.S.A.

Illustrations executed in watercolor on Arches paper.
The type is Bulmer.
Typography and book design by Carol Goldenberg

Library of Congress Cataloging-in-Publication Data
Wiesner, David.
June 29, 1999 / by David Wiesner.
p.   cm.

Summary: While her third-grade classmates are sprouting seeds in
paper cups, Holly has a more ambitious, innovative science project
in mind.
ISBN 0-395-59762-5
[1. Science—Experiments—Fiction.   2. Vegetables—Fiction.]
I. Title.
PZ7.W6367Gr   1992
[E]—dc20   91-34854
                                                      CIP
                                                    AC r92

HOR 10 9 8 7 6 5 4 3 2

JUNE 29, 1999

DAVID WIESNER

CLARION BOOKS · NEW YORK

The place is Ho-Ho-Kus, New Jersey. The year is 1999. On May 11, after months of careful research and planning, Holly Evans launches vegetable seedlings into the sky.

On May 18, the young scientist reports on her experiment. Holly intends to study the effects of extra-terrestrial conditions on vegetable growth and development. She expects the seedlings to stay aloft for several weeks before returning to earth.

Her classmates are speechless.

The date is June 29. Shortly after sunrise, a member of the Billings, Montana, Moose Lodge, hiking through the Rocky Mountains, makes a startling discovery.

Robert Bernabe is in a daze when he returns to camp. All he can say for the next several hours is, "TURNIPS!"

All over the country, the skies fill
with vegetables.

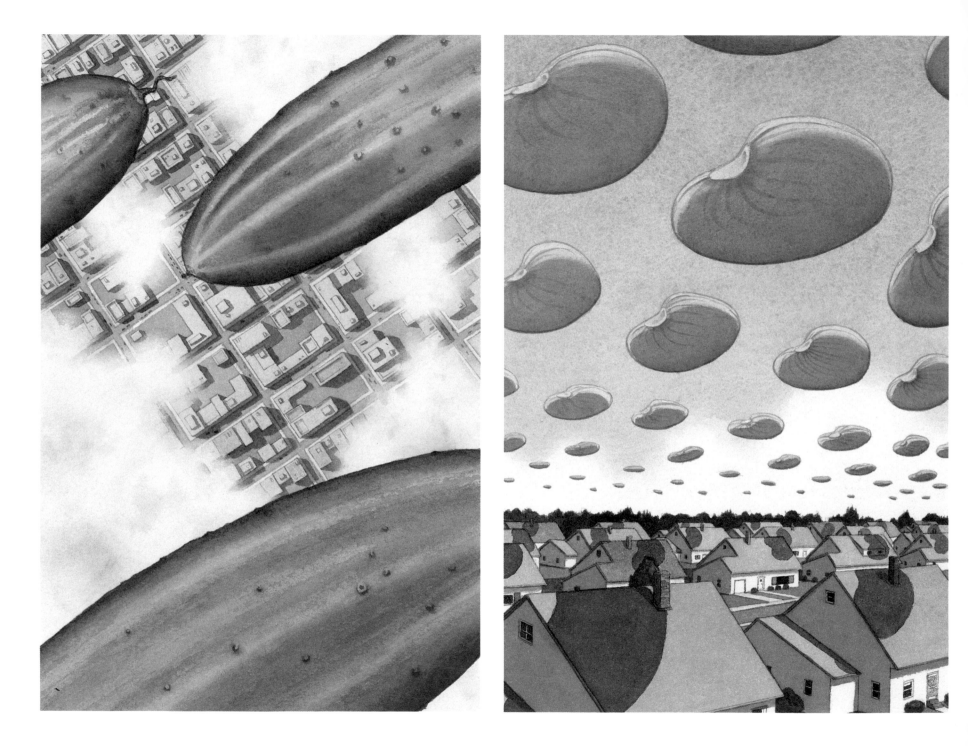

Cucumbers circle Kalamazoo.

Lima beans loom over Levittown.

Artichokes advance on Anchorage.

Parsnips pass by Providence.

And broccoli lands with a big bounce in Holly Evans's backyard.

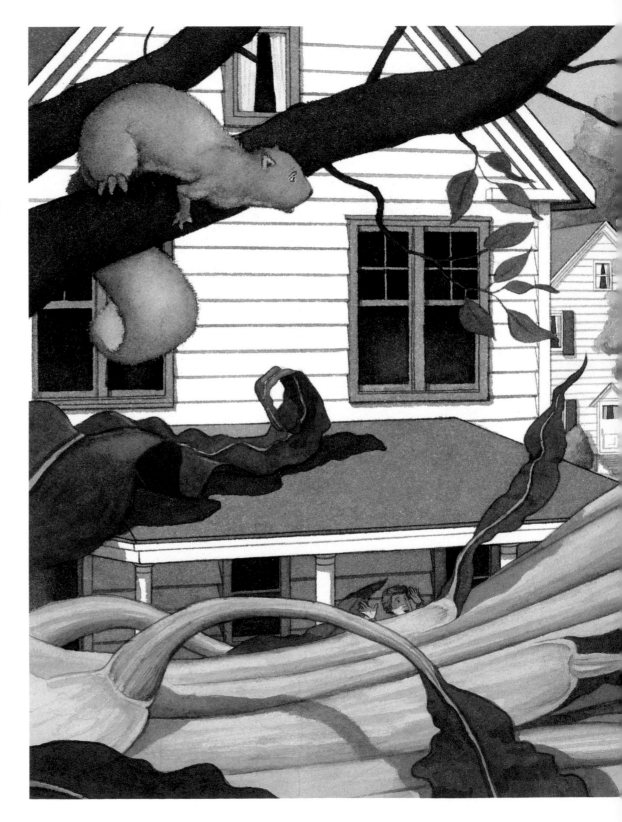

In Ottumwa, Iowa, Tony Kramer emerges from his barn and shouts for joy. "At last, the blue ribbon at the state fair is mine!"

By midafternoon, all vegetables float
safely to the ground.

Except for the peppers. For some reason, they need a little help.

TV news channels broadcast twenty-four-hour coverage of the "airborne vegetal event." Cauliflower carpets California, spinach blankets Greenwich, and arugula covers Ashtabula.

Holly is puzzled. Arugula is not part of her experiment.

Vegetables become very big business. Peas from Peoria are shipped down the Mississippi to Mobile in exchange for eggplant.

Real estate booms in North Carolina.

Avocados bolster Vermont's economy.

Potatoland is wisely abandoned.

The Big Apple is renamed the Big Rutabaga.

Arugula, eggplant, avocado, and now rutabaga. As the list of vegetables that Holly did not plant grows longer, she concludes that the giant specimens are not the results of her experiment.

More curious than disappointed, Holly asks herself, "What happened to *my* vegetables?

"And whose broccoli is in my backyard?"

The place is the ionosphere. On June 29, the Arcturian starcruiser *Alula Borealis* was touring its sixth planet in four days, and the captain had just pointed out the fjords of Norway off the port side.

In the galley an assistant fry cook accidentally jettisoned the entire food supply. As their vegetables drifted toward the small blue planet below, everyone on board had the same thought: Where would their supper come from?